KALEIDOSCOPE

Hurricanes

Joe Thoron

 **Marshall Cavendish**
Benchmark
New York

Marshall Cavendish Benchmark
99 White Plains Road
Tarrytown, New York 10591-9001
www.marshallcavendish.us

Library of Congress Cataloging-in-Publication Data
Thoron, Joe.
Hurricanes / by Joe Thoron.
p. cm. — (Kaleidoscope)
Includes bibliographical references and index.
ISBN-13: 978-0-7614-2103-0 (alk. paper)
ISBN-10: 0-7614-2103-3 (alk. paper)
1. Hurricanes—Juvenile literature. I. Title. II. Series: Kaleidoscope (Marshall Cavendish Benchmark)
QC944.2.T48 2006   551.55'2—dc22   2005017932

Editor: Marilyn Mark
Editorial Director: Michelle Bisson
Art Director: Anahid Hamparian
Series Designer: Adam Mietlowski

Photo Research by Anne Burns Images
Cover Photo by Science Photo Library/NASA

The photographs in this book are used with permission and through the courtesy of: *Corbis*: p. 4 Mike Theiss/Jim Reed Photography; pp. 12, 15, 43 Reuters; p. 19 CIMSS/Sygma; p. 28 Henry Romero/Reuters; p. 35 Bisson Bernard/Sygma; p. 36, 40 Jim Reed; p. 39 Annie Griffiths Belt. *Science Photo Library*: p. 7 NOAA; p. 23 NASA. *NOAA Photo Library*: pp. 8, 20, 31. *Photo Researchers, Inc.*: p. 11 Jim Reed; p. 16 NASA/Science Source. *Associated Press, AP*: pp. 24, 32. *Bridgeman Art Library*: p. 27.

Printed in Malaysia

6 5 4 3 2 1

Contents

Hurricane!

Hurricanes are among the most dramatic and damaging weather events. They destroy buildings, bridges, roads, and power lines. Flying debris breaks windows, and ocean water pushed ahead of the storm sweeps over low-lying areas and knocks down buildings. The heavy rains cause deadly floods where the storm comes ashore and even far inland. The floods from Hurricane Katrina in August 2005 led to more than 1,300 deaths across Louisiana, Mississippi, and Florida. Local economies were hit hard and oil prices across the United States rose drastically almost overnight.

Hurricane Katrina pounds a Fort Lauderdale parking lot in 2005.

A hurricane is a group of intense *thunderstorms* arranged in spiral bands around a calm area in the center, called the *eye*. To be a hurricane, the storm must have winds of over 74 miles per hour (119 kilometers per hour). The strongest hurricanes have winds of over 155 mph (249 kph). An average hurricane is 350 miles (563 km) across, but the largest ones can be up to 900 miles (1,448 km) wide. The eye is usually between 20 and 40 miles (32–64 km) across.

South of the equator, hurricanes are called *typhoons* or *cyclones*. They rotate in a clockwise direction. North of the equator, hurricanes rotate counterclockwise. This happens because of the Earth's rotation, which causes the *Coriolis Effect*, a bending of winds toward or away from the equator. The general term for all of these storms—hurricanes, cyclones, and typhoons—is *tropical cyclone*.

Hurricane Ivan hits the coast of Alabama in 2004. The colors indicate the amount of rain falling. Black and blue areas show the lightest rain. Yellow, orange, and red indicate the heaviest rain.

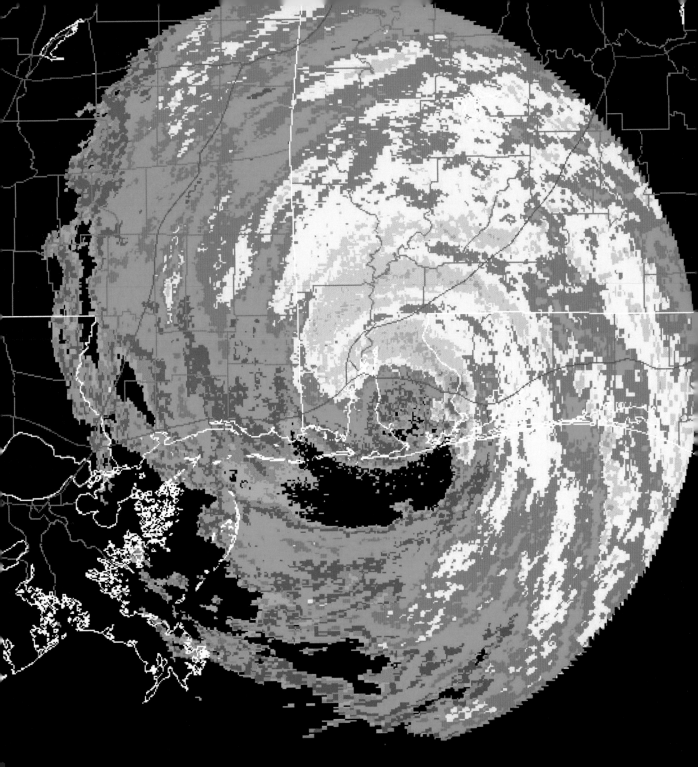

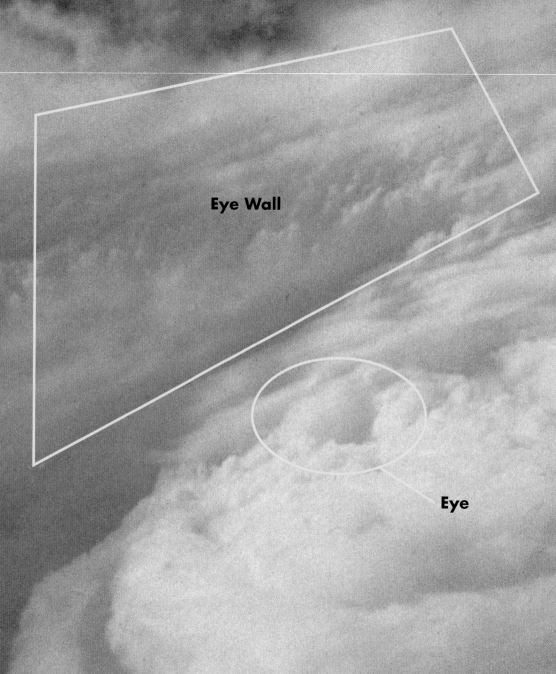

Eye Wall

Eye

The most severe thunderstorms are near the center of the hurricane, surrounding the eye. In this area, called the *eye wall*, air rises rapidly from the surface and then spreads out at high levels of the atmosphere. As the air rises, more air is drawn in to replace it, causing the ferocious winds of the hurricane to spiral toward the center. Seen from the ground or from an airplane, the eye wall is a towering cliff of gray clouds. The clouds can appear almost smooth despite the incredible speeds at which they rotate.

The most intense thunderstorms take place just around the hurricane's eye.

How Hurricanes Form and Die

Hurricanes originate in the *tropics*, slightly to the north or south of the equator. A storm goes through a few stages on the way to becoming a hurricane. The first stage is called a *tropical disturbance*. In this stage, warm, moist ocean air rises from an area of the ocean that is more than 80 degrees Fahrenheit (27 degrees Celsius), which creates an area of low *atmospheric pressure*. As the air rises, it forms thunderstorm clouds.

Storm clouds approach Cape Hatteras, North Carolina, on the eve of Hurricane Isabel in 2003, creating a picturesque sunset.

More air rushes in from the surrounding ocean to replace the rising air. Then, because of the Coriolis Effect, the group of thunderstorms starts to rotate and soon the stormy area earns the title of *tropical depression*. A tropical depression has persistent clouds and thunderstorms, with rotating winds of between 23 and 38 mph (37–61 kph).

Flooding in the Philippines from a tropical depression. While not as severe as hurricanes, tropical depressions can still cause great damage.

If the storm system gathers strength, it becomes a *tropical storm* and is assigned a name. A tropical storm is an organized system of strong thunderstorms with clear rotation and sustained winds of between 39 and 73 mph (63–117 kph), though gusts can be even stronger. If a tropical storm travels over land it can be very damaging. Heavy rainfall causes flooding, and high winds can damage property. In 2001 the flooding from Tropical Storm Allison caused twenty-four fatalities and more than $5 billion in damage to Texas and Louisiana.

When the winds in the storm system reach 74 mph (119 kph) on a sustained basis, the storm has become a hurricane. On average it takes about seven days for a tropical disturbance to become a hurricane.

The city of Houston is at a standstill after Tropical Storm Allison dumped 28 inches of rain in just twenty-four hours. A "state of emergency" was declared in twenty-nine Texas counties after the storm.

Tropical disturbances occur frequently. The Atlantic Ocean has one every few days between June and November each year. Most just fizzle out. On average, fewer than six Atlantic hurricanes occur each year, and not many of those hit land.

Hurricanes only form under special conditions. One of these is weak wind high in the atmosphere. If high level winds are too strong, the gathering storm system gets blown apart instead of growing stronger. Hurricanes start to lose strength when they travel over cooler water or over land. Without the warm ocean air, fewer thunderstorms can form. As a result, the winds slow down and the storm weakens. Over several days or weeks the storm continues to lose power until it is completely gone.

Hurricane Elena, photographed from the space shuttle Discovery *in 1985.*

Hurricane Prediction

Satellites orbiting Earth give *meteorologists* the first glimpses of developing storm systems in the tropics. However, it's hard to predict which storms will develop into hurricanes. It is also hard to predict where a storm might grow more powerful, move faster or slower, or change direction.

Satellite image of Hurricane Mitch as it made landfall in Central America in 1998.

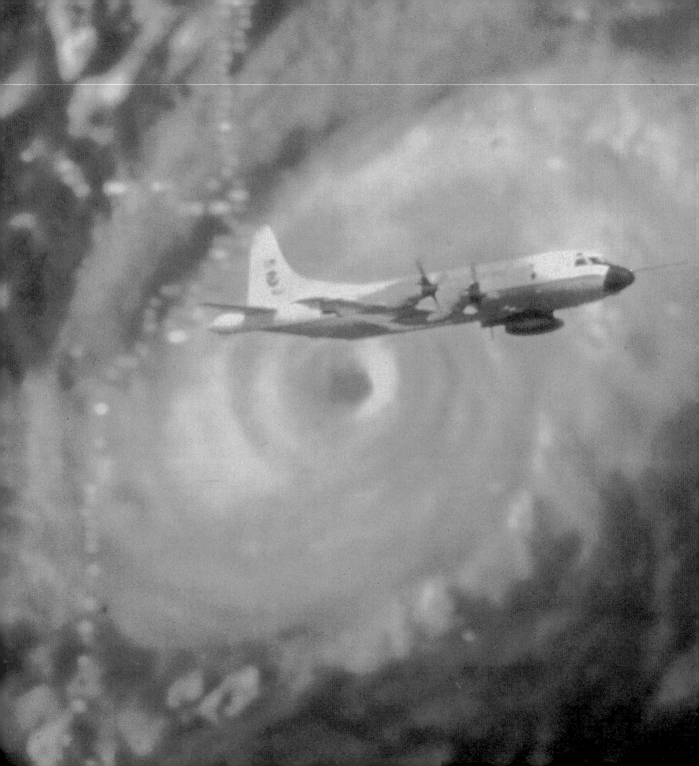

As a storm moves toward land, special "Hurricane Hunter" airplanes fly out toward it. The U.S. Air Force Reserve has a fleet of aircraft that fly directly into the center of the storm. They take measurements of the conditions at flight level and drop special equipment into the storm to measure wind strength, *air pressure*, *humidity*, and *temperature*. Among the most important pieces of information forecasters need are the wind speeds at the surface, because this wind will do the most damage when the hurricane hits land. The National Oceanic and Atmospheric Administration (NOAA) also flies planes into hurricanes. These missions focus on understanding how hurricanes form, gather strength, and move, in order to make better predictions about future storms.

Hurricane hunter airplanes like this NOAA P-3 make dangerous missions into the middle of hurricanes to learn more about them.

Closer to land, *Doppler radar* installations can peer into the approaching storm, giving forecasters the information needed to provide accurate short-term forecasts for floods and high winds.

Once the information is gathered, it is then plugged into sophisticated computer models that help forecasters determine where the storm might come ashore, how strong it will be, and how much rain will fall. Unfortunately, hurricanes are quite unpredictable. They start and stop, weave and wiggle. Scientists have compared their motion to that of a fallen leaf being carried along on the surface of a stream.

A computer-generated hurricane crosses the Gulf of Mexico. Computer models help scientists predict the path and the severity of real hurricanes.

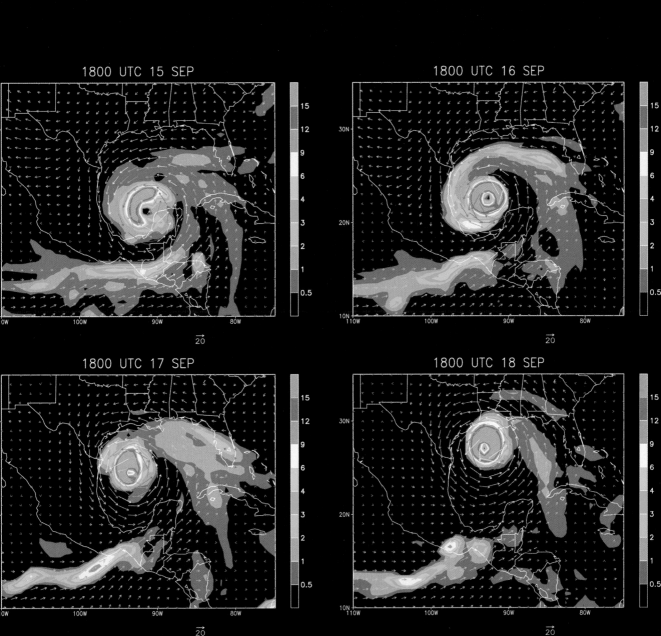

Though forecasts of storm tracks are now twice as accurate as they were in 1970, forecasters have not become much better at gauging how intense a hurricane will be when it hits land. More research must be done to improve future forecasts.

Forecasters at the National Hurricane Center huddle over a computer screen showing Hurricane Lili, which hit Louisiana in October 2002.

Damage from Wind and Water

Hurricanes injure and kill many people each year, damaging the property and economies of the regions they hit. Some hurricanes have even affected the course of world history. In 1281 Kublai Khan's huge fleet was sunk by a typhoon, preventing him from conquering Japan and making the country part of the Mongol Empire. In 1588 two weakening hurricanes destroyed most of the Spanish Armada during Spain's attempt to invade England. As a result, England was saved from invasion and its navy gained control of the sea.

The Spanish Armada, painted in 1588 by Nicholas Hilliard (1547–1619).

Hurricane damage comes from two main sources: wind and water. The winds of a Category 1 hurricane, blowing at 74 to 95 mph (119–153 kph), can damage mobile homes, shrubbery, and trees. As the wind speed rises, devastation becomes more severe. With winds of 111 to 130 mph (179–209 kph), a Category 3 hurricane can demolish mobile homes and damage wooden houses. A Category 5 hurricane has winds of over 155 mph (249 kph). These winds can rip roofs off most buildings and destroy even sturdy structures.

Hurricane damage from Ivan on the coast of Cuba, 2004.

Hurricane winds are not consistent, and gusts can be much stronger than the average wind speed. Researchers have found that small areas of especially intense winds sometimes develop inside a storm. When Hurricane Andrew hit southern Florida in 1992, some of the worst damage was done by strong whirlwinds—about 10 miles (16 km) across—near the eye wall. Winds in these whirlwinds reached 200 mph (322 kph).

The intense thunderstorms that make up a hurricane can also spawn *tornadoes*, adding to the devastation caused by wind. The tornadoes set off by Hurricane Katrina in 2005 hit as far away as Georgia.

Tornadoes created by Hurricane Andrew destroyed these buildings in La Place, Louisiana.

Damage from water comes from both rainfall and the storm surge of the ocean. An average hurricane dumps 6 to 12 inches (15–30 centimeters) of rain on the land below it. The rainfall from Hurricane Katrina in 2005 exceeded rates of 1 inch (2.5 cm) per hour as it hit the Gulf Coast, and flooding caused by a damaged levee on nearby Lake Pontchartrain left 80 percent of New Orleans under water. Rains from hurricanes cause creeks and rivers to flood and mud slides can also form, even far inland from the area in which the hurricane first comes ashore. In 1969 Hurricane Camille dumped 9.8 inches (24.9 cm) of rain on Virginia's Blue Ridge Mountains after it had curved across Mississippi, Tennessee, Kentucky, and West Virginia.

Hurricane Katrina's fierce winds and flooding ruined this New Orleans home and these vehicles. Hundreds of thousands of homes and vehicles in Louisiana were destroyed.

In the past thirty years, most hurricane deaths in the United States have come from inland flooding rather than from wind. The problem is the same around the world. In 1995 Hurricane Mitch deposited an estimated 75 inches (that's more than 6 feet!) of rain on some mountain areas of Honduras. Flooding and mud slides from Mitch killed more than 11,000 people.

Hurricane Mitch caused devastating flooding in Central America.

▶

Storm surge is one of the most damaging effects of a hurricane along the coast. A storm surge is a raised area of water some 50 or more miles (80 km) wide. It is created by three factors. First, most of the height of the surge (about 85 percent) comes from fierce hurricane winds. These winds create large waves that can build up into an area of water that is 19 to 33 feet (6–10 m) higher than usual. Second, the low atmospheric pressure of the storm actually makes the sea level rise in the area of the eye. It can rise to about 3 feet (0.9 m) higher than usual. The third factor is the shape of the coast itself, which can create a surge. As the mass of water moves into shallower areas, the waves grow steeper and higher. If the storm surge comes ashore during a high tide, the effect is even worse.

A Cape Hatteras motorist is trapped by waves surging over a state highway during the landfall of Hurricane Isabel. Within a few hours, the highway was completely destroyed.

Water is incredibly powerful. One cubic foot of water weighs 62.4 pounds (28.3 kilograms). Waves sweep over the land and then draw back, knocking down structures and then ripping them apart. In many areas of the coastal United States, people live along the shore. It does not take a big rise in the ocean level to destroy their homes. In some storms, like the Category 5 Hurricane Camille in Mississippi in 1969, the storm surge can be as high as 25 feet (8 m).

Large waves from Hurricane Felix slam evacuated beach houses on Virginia Beach in 1995.

Hurricane Safety

The key to staying safe in a hurricane is preparation. Create a safety plan with your family. Know the risks for your area, such as storm surges and flooding, and the routes to safe inland locations. Create a stockpile of nonperishable food and fresh water, and a disaster kit containing first-aid items, clothing, sleeping bags, flashlights, a radio, and some cash.

The National Weather Service (NWS) provides two kinds of hurricane alerts. A *hurricane watch* means a hurricane may be coming your way. If a hurricane watch is announced for your area, prepare to evacuate. Cover windows and doors with plywood, bring all lightweight items inside, and gather supplies to take with you.

Workers board up store windows in preparation for Hurricane Fran at Myrtle Beach in 1996.

A *hurricane warning* means forecasters expect a hurricane to strike your area soon. When the hurricane watch in your area becomes a warning, stay tuned to radio or television reports and be ready to leave as soon as local officials give an evacuation order.

If you must stay home during a hurricane, turn off all appliances and propane tanks, and take shelter in an interior room or hallway on the first floor. If the eye passes over you, don't go outside!

Residents flee from Cocoa Beach, Florida, in 1999, as Hurricane Floyd approaches.

▶

Glossary

air pressure—A nonscientific term for atmospheric pressure.

atmospheric pressure—The pressure exerted by Earth's atmosphere at any particular point. Also called barometric pressure.

Coriolis Effect—The effect of the Earth's rotation on airborne objects, including wind. This effect makes winds blowing toward the equator curve to the west and winds blowing away from it curve east.

cyclone—An area of low pressure around which winds blow in a circular pattern; also, the term used for a hurricane located in the Indian Ocean or in the Western Pacific Ocean.

Doppler radar—A radar system used for determining the speed of a moving object.

eye—The center of a hurricane, which is an area of relative calm and low atmospheric pressure.

eye wall—The band of extremely violent thunderstorms surrounding a hurricane's eye.

humidity—The amount of moisture in the air.

hurricane warning—A serious warning from the National Weather Service (NWS) that a hurricane is expected to reach a certain area very soon.

hurricane watch—A notice from the National Weather Service (NWS) that a hurricane might strike a certain area.

meteorologists—People who study the atmosphere, including the weather and the climate.

thunderstorms—Storms of lightning and thunder, usually with rain and gusty winds.

tornado—A destructive whirlwind that forms underneath some violent thunderstorms.

tropical cyclone—The general term for a hurricane, typhoon, or cyclone.

tropical depression—A group of rotating thunderstorms with winds between 23 and 38 miles (37–61 km) per hour.

tropical disturbance—A group of thunderstorms over the ocean with winds of less than 23 miles (37 km) per hour.

tropical storm—A rotating group of thunderstorms with winds between 39 and 73 miles (63–117 km) per hour.

tropics—The region on either side of the equator between the Tropic of Cancer (23-1/2 degrees north) and the Tropic of Capricorn (23-1/2 degrees south).

typhoon—Tropical cyclones in the western Pacific Ocean or near India.

Find Out More

Books

Chambers, Catherine. *Hurricane*. Chicago: Heinemann Library, 2002.

Morris, Neil. *Hurricanes & Tornadoes*. New York: Crabtree Publishing, 1998.

Simon, Seymour. *Hurricanes*. New York: HarperCollins Juvenile Books, 2003.

Web Sites

Information about Hurricane Katrina
http://www.ncdc.noaa.gov/oa/climate/research/2005/katrina.html

The National Oceanic and Atmospheric Administration (NOAA)
http://www.education.noaa.gov/
http://hurricanes.noaa.gov/

Other Hurricane Sites
http://www.miamisci.org/hurricane/
http://www.ucar.edu/educ_outreach/webweather/
http://weatherwizkids.com/hurricane1.htm

About the Author

Joe Thoron is a freelance writer in Washington state. When not writing for children, he builds Web sites and writes marketing copy. He lives on an island north of Seattle, right between several sleeping volcanoes and a major earthquake zone.

Index

Page numbers for illustrations are in **boldface.**